DOROTHY AND THE WIZARD IN OZ

VOL. 3

ADAPTED FROM
THE BOOK BY
L. FRANK BAUM

Writer: **ERIC SHANOWER**

Artist: **SKOTTIE YOUNG**

Colorist: **JEAN-FRANCOIS BEAULIEU**

Letterer: **JEFF ECKLEBERRY**

Assistant Editors: **RACHEL PINNELAS & JON MOISAN**

Editor: **SANA AMANAT**

Collection Editor: **MARK D. BEAZLEY**

Assistant Editors: **NELSON RIBEIRO & ALEX STARBUCK**

Editor, Special Projects: **JENNIFER GRÜNWALD**

Senior Editor, Special Projects: **JEFF YOUNGQUIST**

Senior Vice President Print, Sales & Marketing: **DAVID GABRIEL**

Editor in Chief: **AXEL ALONSO**

Chief Creative Officer: **JOE QUESADA**

Publisher: **DAN BUCKLEY**

Executive Producer: **ALAN FINE**

ABDO
Spotlight

ABDOPUBLISHING.COM

Reinforced library bound edition published in 2015 by Spotlight,
a division of ABDO, PO Box 398166, Minneapolis, Minnesota 55439.
Spotlight produces high-quality reinforced library bound editions for
schools and libraries. Published by agreement with Marvel Characters, Inc.

Printed in the United States of America, North Mankato, Minnesota.
112014
012015

THIS BOOK CONTAINS
RECYCLED MATERIALS

Marvel.com
© 2014 Marvel

LIBRARY OF CONGRESS CATALOGING-IN-PUBLICATION DATA

Shanower, Eric.
   Dorothy and the Wizard in Oz / adapted from the novel by L. Frank Baum ;
writer: Eric Shanower ; artist: Skottie Young. -- Reinforced library bound
edition.
       pages cm
   "Marvel."
   Summary: During a California earthquake Dorothy falls into the
underground Land of the Mangaboos where she again meets the Wizard of
Oz.
   ISBN 978-1-61479-343-4 (vol. 1) -- ISBN 978-1-61479-344-1 (vol. 2) -- ISBN
978-1-61479-345-8 (vol. 3) -- ISBN 978-1-61479-346-5 (vol. 4) -- ISBN 978-1-
61479-347-2 (vol. 5) -- ISBN 978-1-61479-348-9 (vol. 6) -- ISBN 978-1-61479-
349-6 (vol. 7) -- ISBN 978-1-61479-350-2 (vol. 8)
   1. Graphic novels. [1. Graphic novels. 2. Fantasy.] I. Young, Skottie,
illustrator. II. Baum, L. Frank (Lyman Frank), 1856-1919. Dorothy and the
Wizard in Oz. III. Title.
   PZ7.7.S453Dor 2015
   741.5'973--dc23
                         2014033625

Spotlight

A Division of ABDO
abdopublishing.com

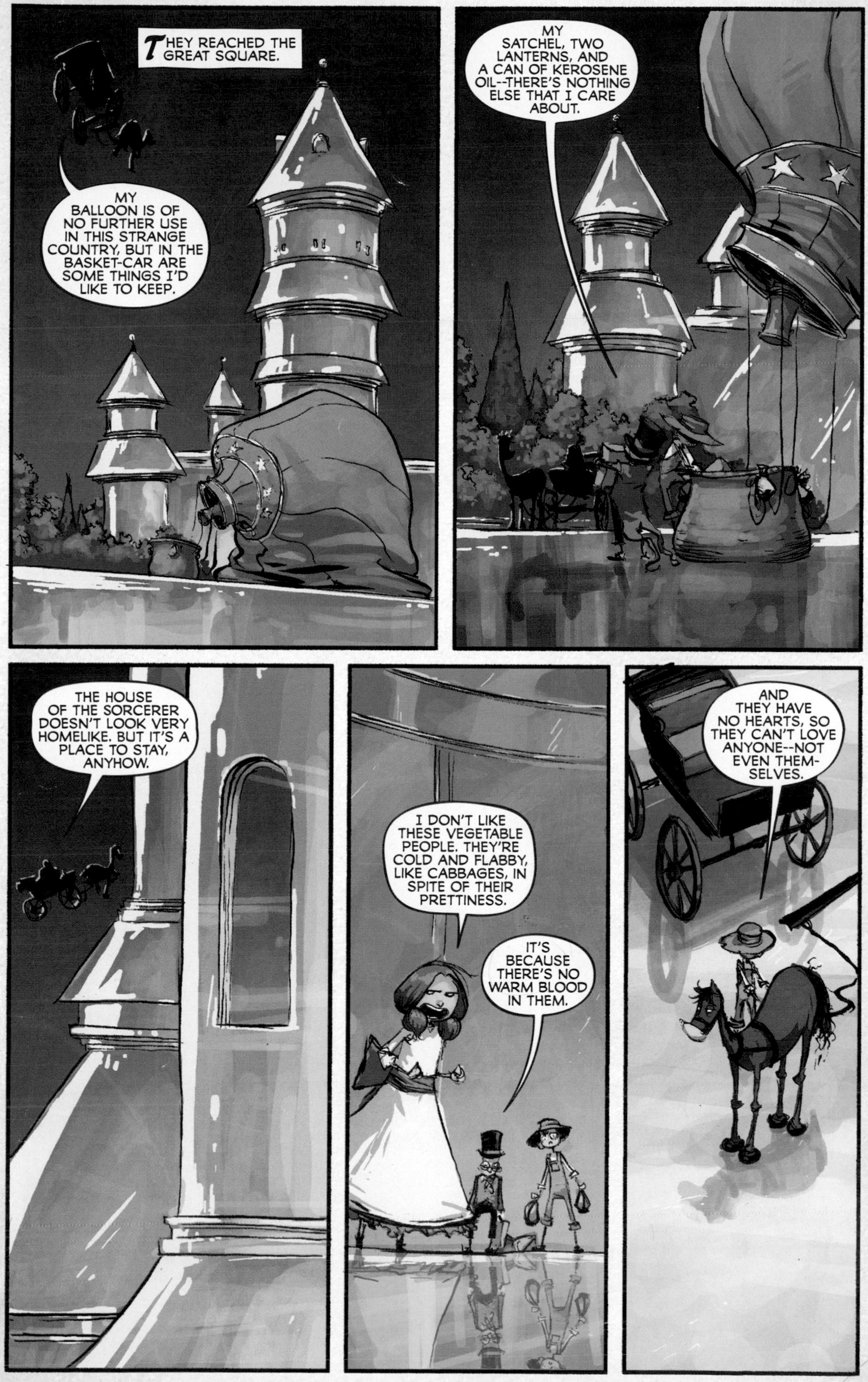
THEY REACHED THE GREAT SQUARE.
MY BALLOON IS OF NO FURTHER USE IN THIS STRANGE COUNTRY, BUT IN THE BASKET-CAR ARE SOME THINGS I'D LIKE TO KEEP.
MY SATCHEL, TWO LANTERNS, AND A CAN OF KEROSENE OIL--THERE'S NOTHING ELSE THAT I CARE ABOUT.
THE HOUSE OF THE SORCERER DOESN'T LOOK VERY HOMELIKE. BUT IT'S A PLACE TO STAY, ANYHOW.
I DON'T LIKE THESE VEGETABLE PEOPLE. THEY'RE COLD AND FLABBY, LIKE CABBAGES, IN SPITE OF THEIR PRETTINESS.
IT'S BECAUSE THERE'S NO WARM BLOOD IN THEM.
AND THEY HAVE NO HEARTS, SO THEY CAN'T LOVE ANYONE--NOT EVEN THEM-SELVES.

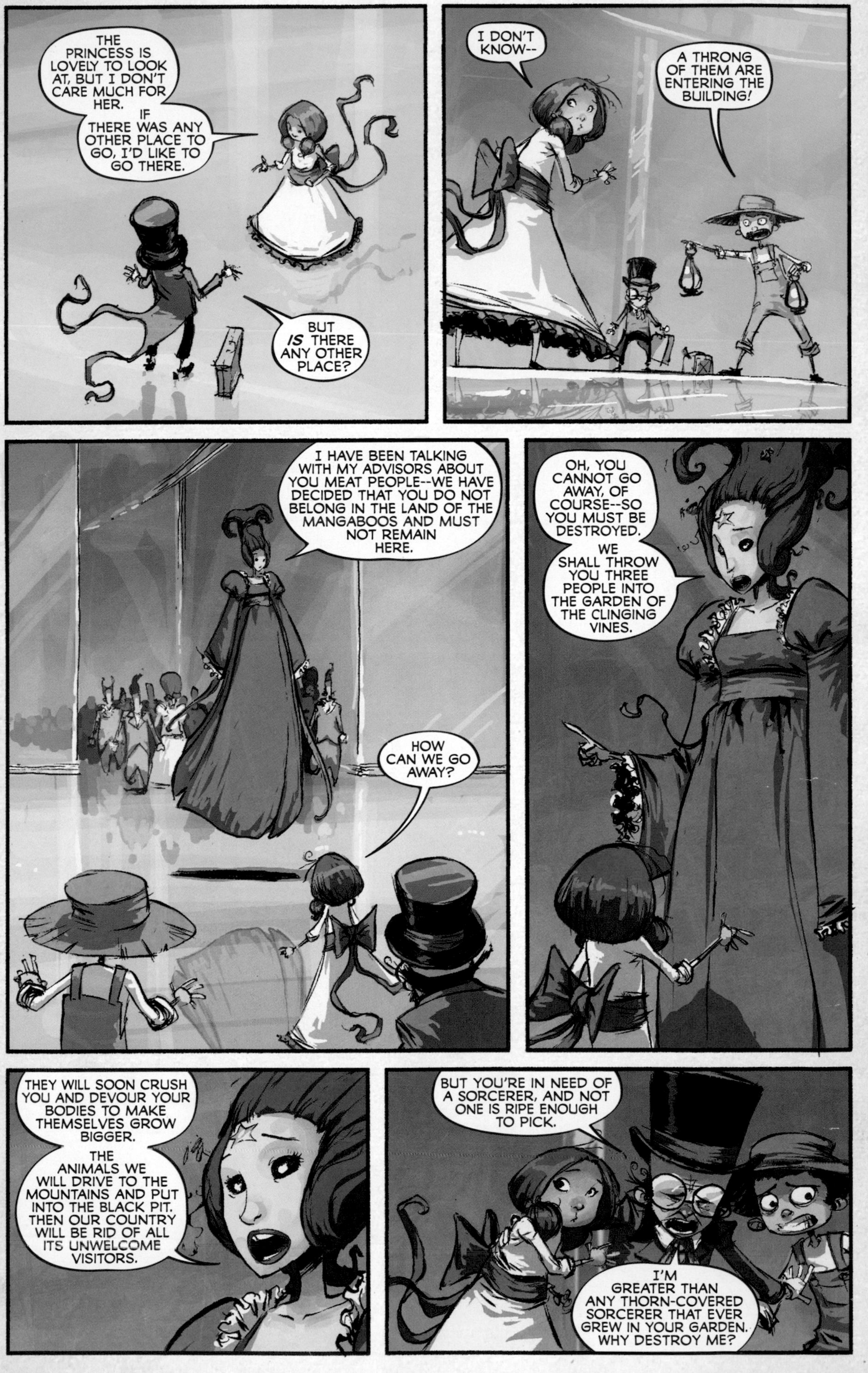
THE PRINCESS IS LOVELY TO LOOK AT, BUT I DON'T CARE MUCH FOR HER.
IF THERE WAS ANY OTHER PLACE TO GO, I'D LIKE TO GO THERE.
BUT *IS* THERE ANY OTHER PLACE?
I DON'T KNOW--
A THRONG OF THEM ARE ENTERING THE BUILDING!
I HAVE BEEN TALKING WITH MY ADVISORS ABOUT YOU MEAT PEOPLE--WE HAVE DECIDED THAT YOU DO NOT BELONG IN THE LAND OF THE MANGABOOS AND MUST NOT REMAIN HERE.
HOW CAN WE GO AWAY?
OH, YOU CANNOT GO AWAY, OF COURSE--SO YOU MUST BE DESTROYED.
WE SHALL THROW YOU THREE PEOPLE INTO THE GARDEN OF THE CLINGING VINES.
THEY WILL SOON CRUSH YOU AND DEVOUR YOUR BODIES TO MAKE THEMSELVES GROW BIGGER.
THE ANIMALS WE WILL DRIVE TO THE MOUNTAINS AND PUT INTO THE BLACK PIT. THEN OUR COUNTRY WILL BE RID OF ALL ITS UNWELCOME VISITORS.
BUT YOU'RE IN NEED OF A SORCERER, AND NOT ONE IS RIPE ENOUGH TO PICK.
I'M GREATER THAN ANY THORN-COVERED SORCERER THAT EVER GREW IN YOUR GARDEN. WHY DESTROY ME?

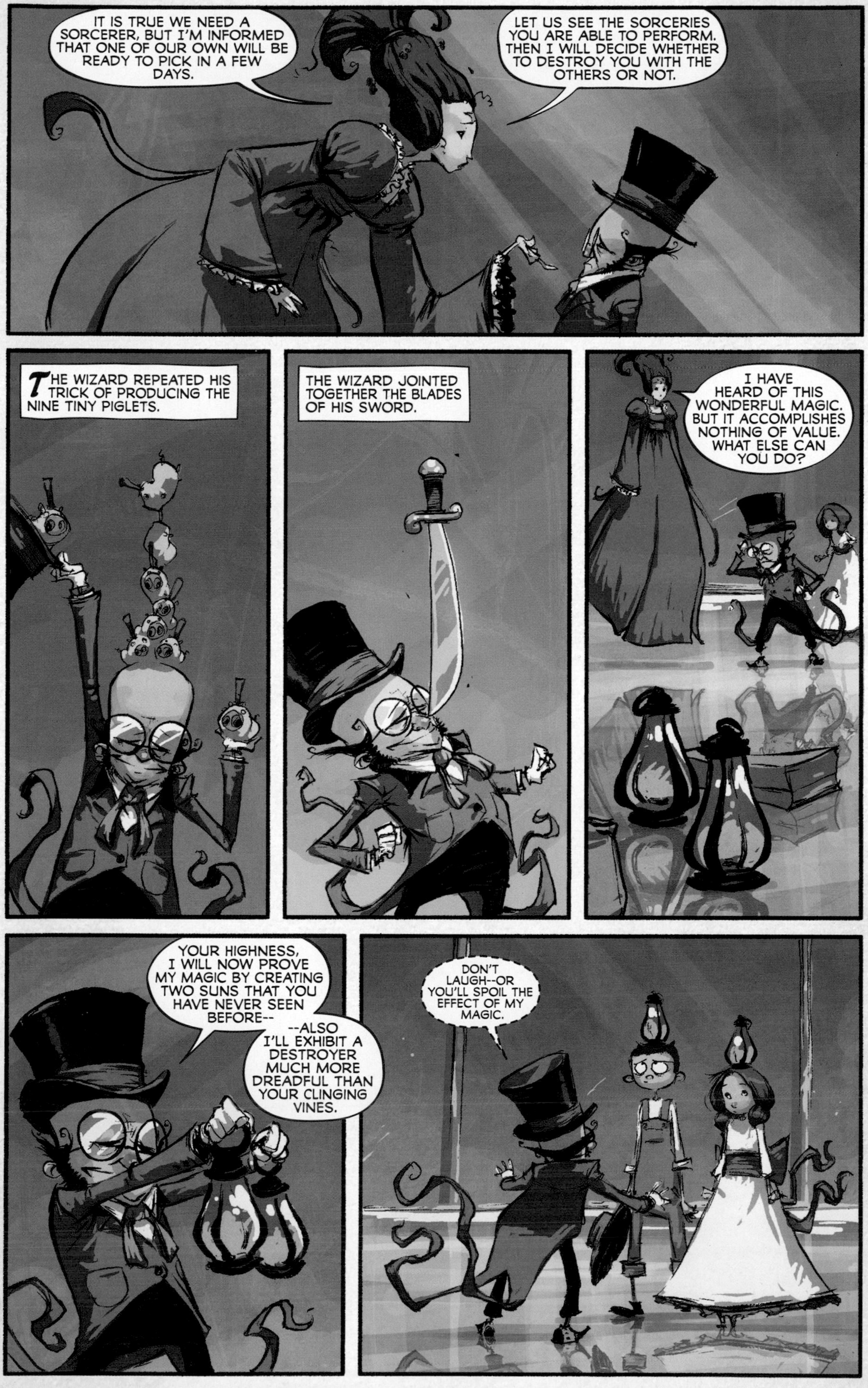
IT IS TRUE WE NEED A SORCERER, BUT I'M INFORMED THAT ONE OF OUR OWN WILL BE READY TO PICK IN A FEW DAYS.
LET US SEE THE SORCERIES YOU ARE ABLE TO PERFORM. THEN I WILL DECIDE WHETHER TO DESTROY YOU WITH THE OTHERS OR NOT.
THE WIZARD REPEATED HIS TRICK OF PRODUCING THE NINE TINY PIGLETS.
THE WIZARD JOINTED TOGETHER THE BLADES OF HIS SWORD.
I HAVE HEARD OF THIS WONDERFUL MAGIC. BUT IT ACCOMPLISHES NOTHING OF VALUE. WHAT ELSE CAN YOU DO?
YOUR HIGHNESS, I WILL NOW PROVE MY MAGIC BY CREATING TWO SUNS THAT YOU HAVE NEVER SEEN BEFORE--
--ALSO I'LL EXHIBIT A DESTROYER MUCH MORE DREADFUL THAN YOUR CLINGING VINES.
DON'T LAUGH--OR YOU'LL SPOIL THE EFFECT OF MY MAGIC.

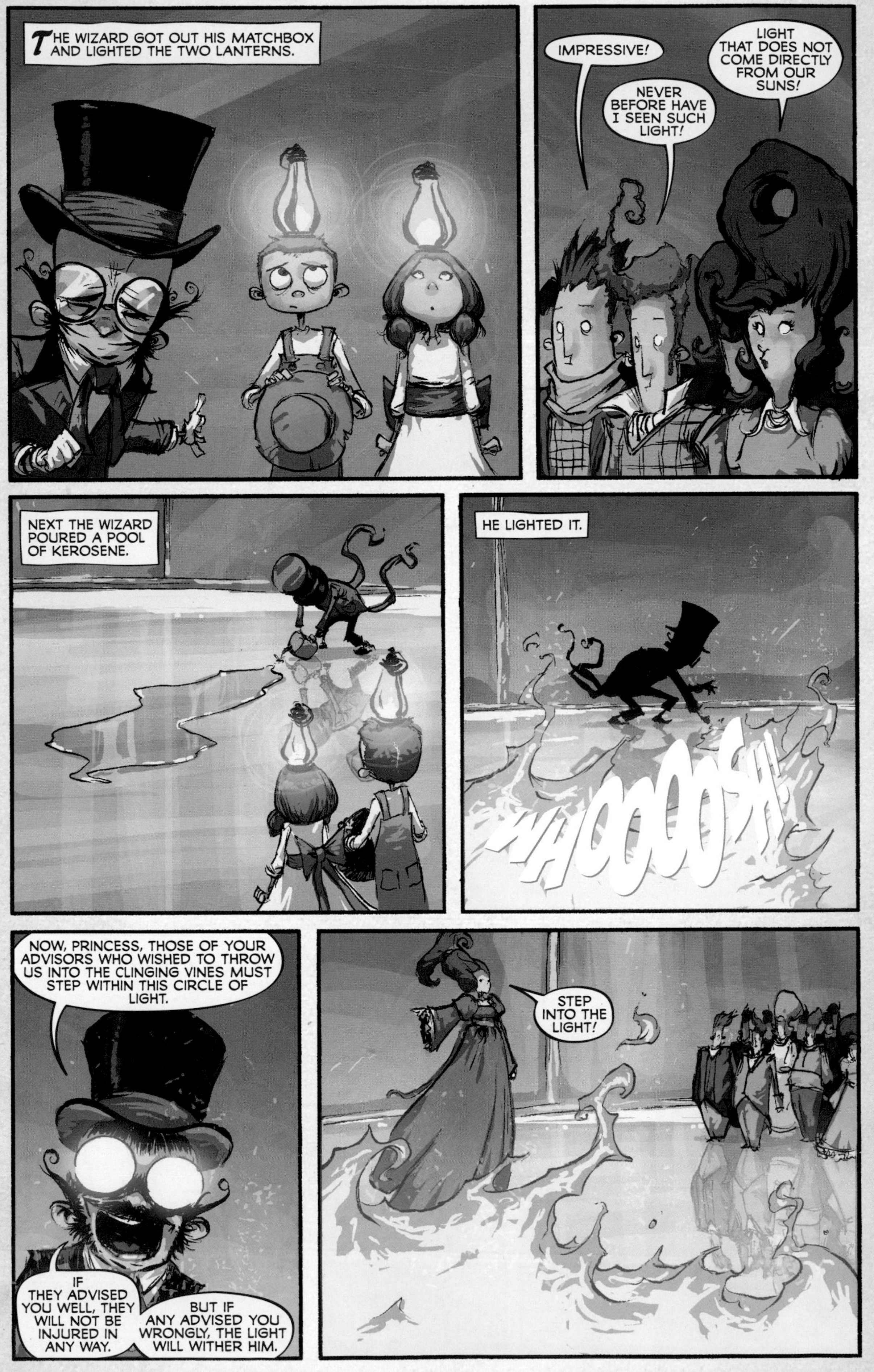
THE WIZARD GOT OUT HIS MATCHBOX AND LIGHTED THE TWO LANTERNS.
IMPRESSIVE!
NEVER BEFORE HAVE I SEEN SUCH LIGHT!
LIGHT THAT DOES NOT COME DIRECTLY FROM OUR SUNS!
NEXT THE WIZARD POURED A POOL OF KEROSENE.
HE LIGHTED IT.
WHOOOOSH!
NOW, PRINCESS, THOSE OF YOUR ADVISORS WHO WISHED TO THROW US INTO THE CLINGING VINES MUST STEP WITHIN THIS CIRCLE OF LIGHT.
IF THEY ADVISED YOU WELL, THEY WILL NOT BE INJURED IN ANY WAY.
BUT IF ANY ADVISED YOU WRONGLY, THE LIGHT WILL WITHER HIM.
STEP INTO THE LIGHT!

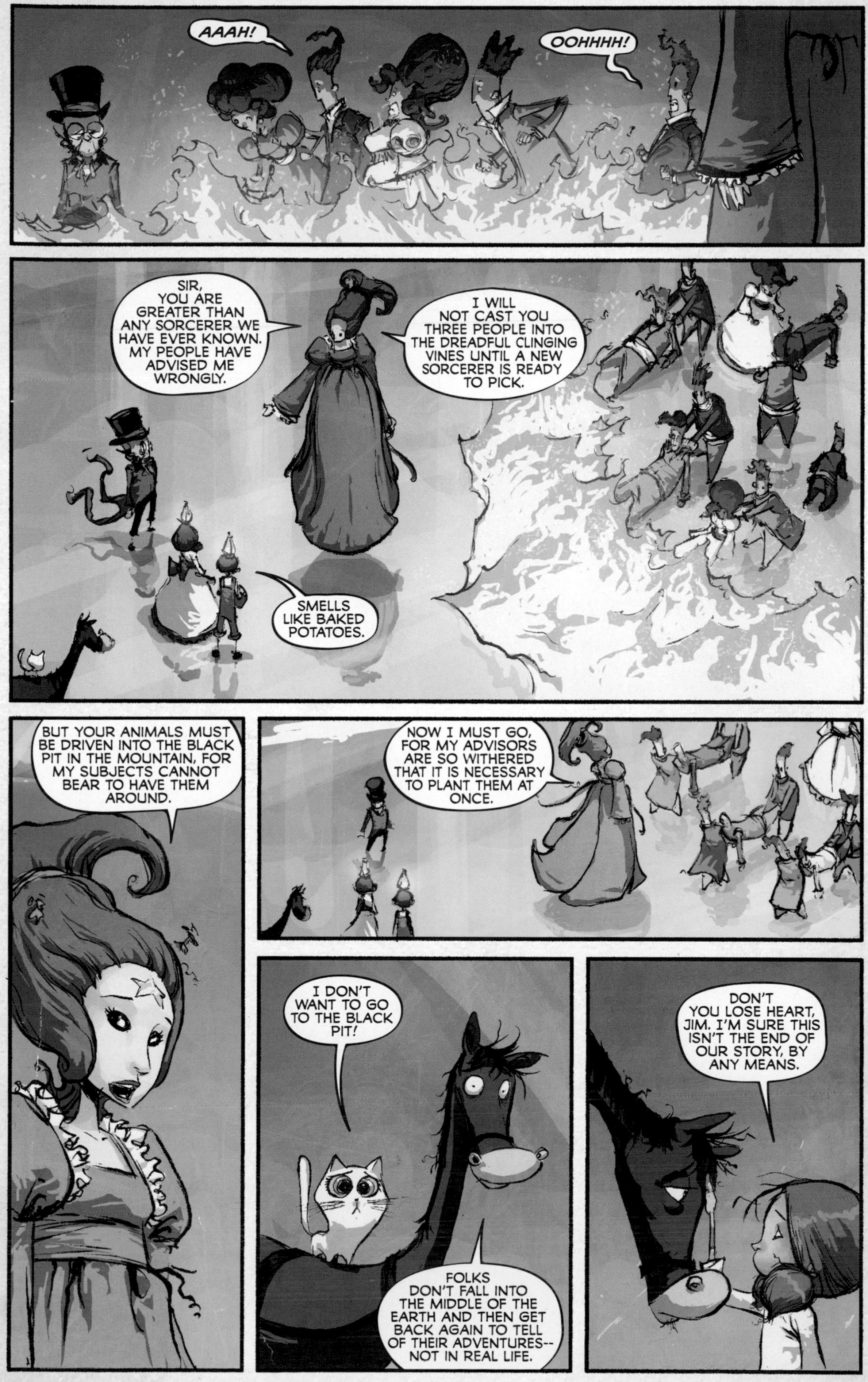
AAAH!
OOHHHH!
SIR, YOU ARE GREATER THAN ANY SORCERER WE HAVE EVER KNOWN. MY PEOPLE HAVE ADVISED ME WRONGLY.
I WILL NOT CAST YOU THREE PEOPLE INTO THE DREADFUL CLINGING VINES UNTIL A NEW SORCERER IS READY TO PICK.
SMELLS LIKE BAKED POTATOES.
BUT YOUR ANIMALS MUST BE DRIVEN INTO THE MOUNTAIN, FOR MY SUBJECTS CANNOT BEAR TO HAVE THEM AROUND.
NOW I MUST GO, FOR MY ADVISORS ARE SO WITHERED THAT IT IS NECESSARY TO PLANT THEM AT ONCE.
I DON'T WANT TO GO TO THE BLACK PIT!
FOLKS DON'T FALL INTO THE MIDDLE OF THE EARTH AND THEN GET BACK AGAIN TO TELL OF THEIR ADVENTURES-- NOT IN REAL LIFE.
DON'T YOU LOSE HEART, JIM. I'M SURE THIS ISN'T THE END OF OUR STORY, BY ANY MEANS.

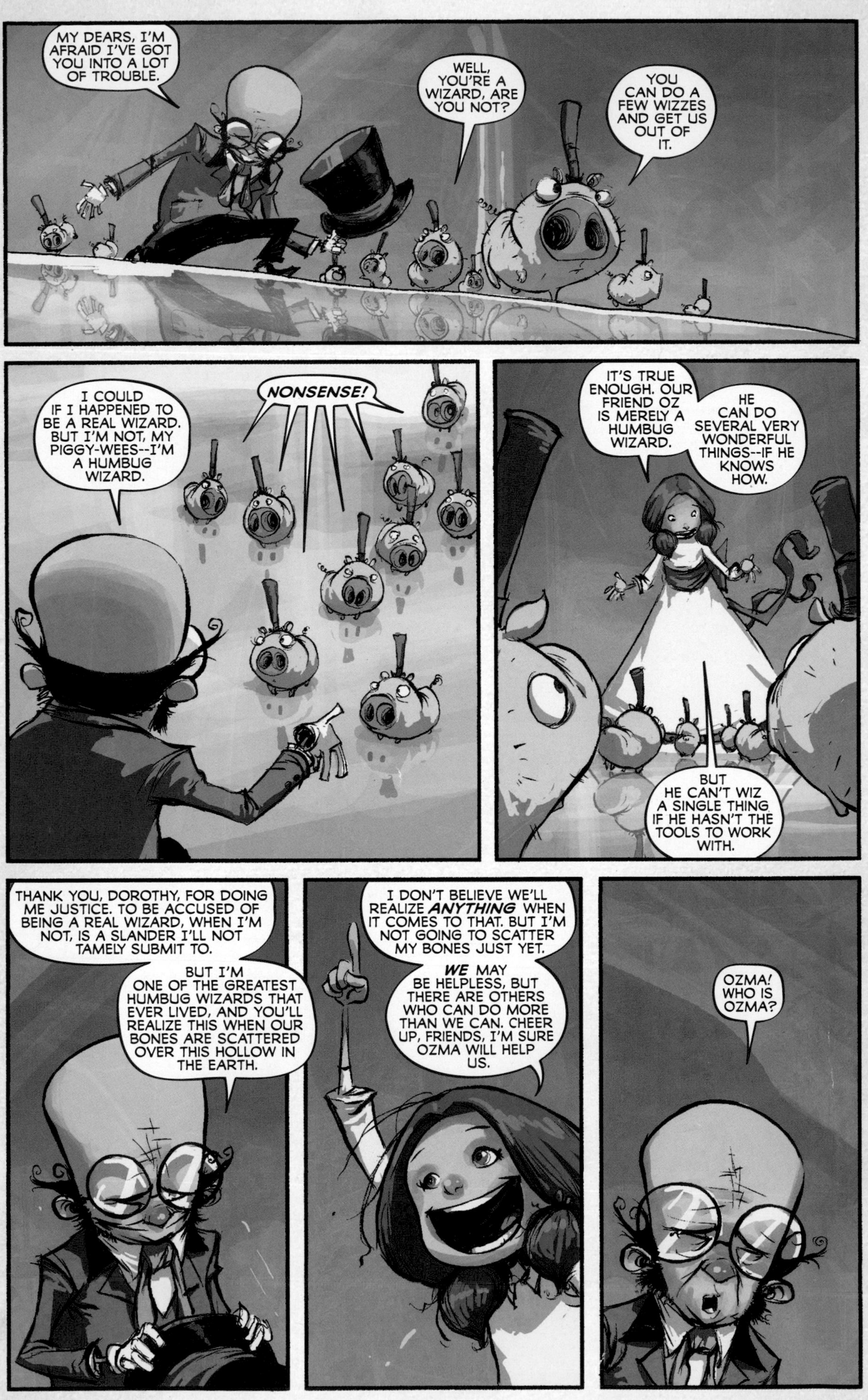
MY DEARS, I'M AFRAID I'VE GOT YOU INTO A LOT OF TROUBLE.
WELL, YOU'RE A WIZARD, ARE YOU NOT?
YOU CAN DO A FEW WIZZES AND GET US OUT OF IT.
I COULD IF I HAPPENED TO BE A REAL WIZARD. BUT I'M NOT, MY PIGGY-WEES--I'M A HUMBUG WIZARD.
NONSENSE!
IT'S TRUE ENOUGH. OUR FRIEND OZ IS MERELY A HUMBUG WIZARD.
HE CAN DO SEVERAL VERY WONDERFUL THINGS--IF HE KNOWS HOW.
BUT HE CAN'T WIZ A SINGLE THING IF HE HASN'T THE TOOLS TO WORK WITH.
THANK YOU, DOROTHY, FOR DOING ME JUSTICE. TO BE ACCUSED OF BEING A REAL WIZARD, WHEN I'M NOT, IS A SLANDER I'LL NOT TAMELY SUBMIT TO.
BUT I'M ONE OF THE GREATEST HUMBUG WIZARDS THAT EVER LIVED, AND YOU'LL REALIZE THIS WHEN OUR BONES ARE SCATTERED OVER THIS HOLLOW IN THE EARTH.
I DON'T BELIEVE WE'LL REALIZE ANYTHING WHEN IT COMES TO THAT. BUT I'M NOT GOING TO SCATTER MY BONES JUST YET.
WE MAY BE HELPLESS, BUT THERE ARE OTHERS WHO CAN DO MORE THAN WE CAN. CHEER UP, FRIENDS, I'M SURE OZMA WILL HELP US.
OZMA! WHO IS OZMA?

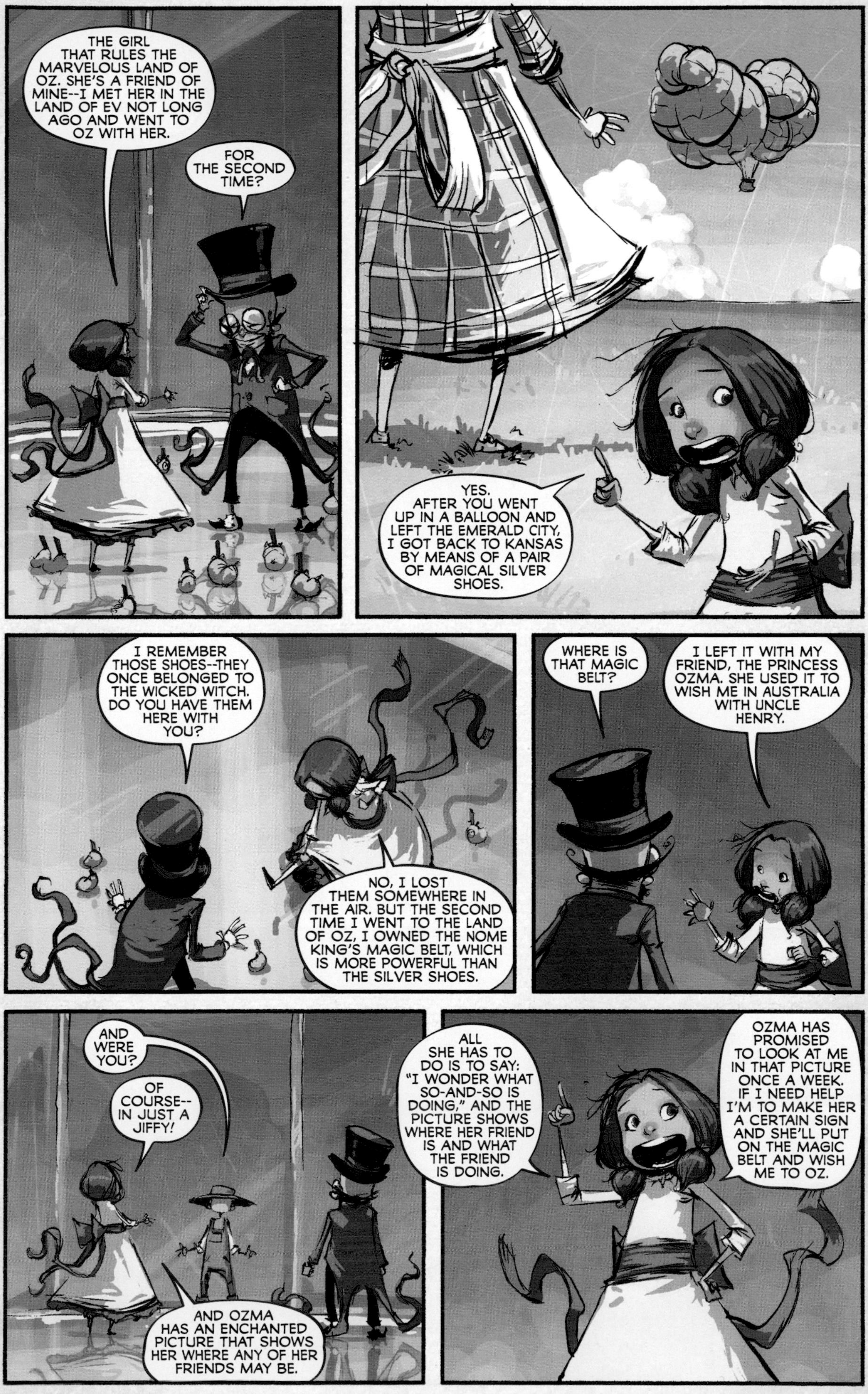
THE GIRL THAT RULES THE MARVELOUS LAND OF OZ. SHE'S A FRIEND OF MINE--I MET HER IN THE LAND OF EV NOT LONG AGO AND WENT TO OZ WITH HER.
FOR THE SECOND TIME?
YES. AFTER YOU WENT UP IN A BALLOON AND LEFT THE EMERALD CITY, I GOT BACK TO KANSAS BY MEANS OF A PAIR OF MAGICAL SILVER SHOES.
I REMEMBER THOSE SHOES--THEY ONCE BELONGED TO THE WICKED WITCH. DO YOU HAVE THEM HERE WITH YOU?
NO, I LOST THEM SOMEWHERE IN THE AIR. BUT THE SECOND TIME I WENT TO THE LAND OF OZ, I OWNED THE NOME KING'S MAGIC BELT, WHICH IS MORE POWERFUL THAN THE SILVER SHOES.
WHERE IS THAT MAGIC BELT?
I LEFT IT WITH MY FRIEND, THE PRINCESS OZMA. SHE USED IT TO WISH ME IN AUSTRALIA WITH UNCLE HENRY.
AND WERE YOU?
OF COURSE--IN JUST A JIFFY!
AND OZMA HAS AN ENCHANTED PICTURE THAT SHOWS HER WHERE ANY OF HER FRIENDS MAY BE.
ALL SHE HAS TO DO IS TO SAY: "I WONDER WHAT SO-AND-SO IS DOING," AND THE PICTURE SHOWS WHERE HER FRIEND IS AND WHAT THE FRIEND IS DOING.
OZMA HAS PROMISED TO LOOK AT ME IN THAT PICTURE ONCE A WEEK. IF I NEED HELP I'M TO MAKE HER A CERTAIN SIGN AND SHE'LL PUT ON THE MAGIC BELT AND WISH ME TO OZ.

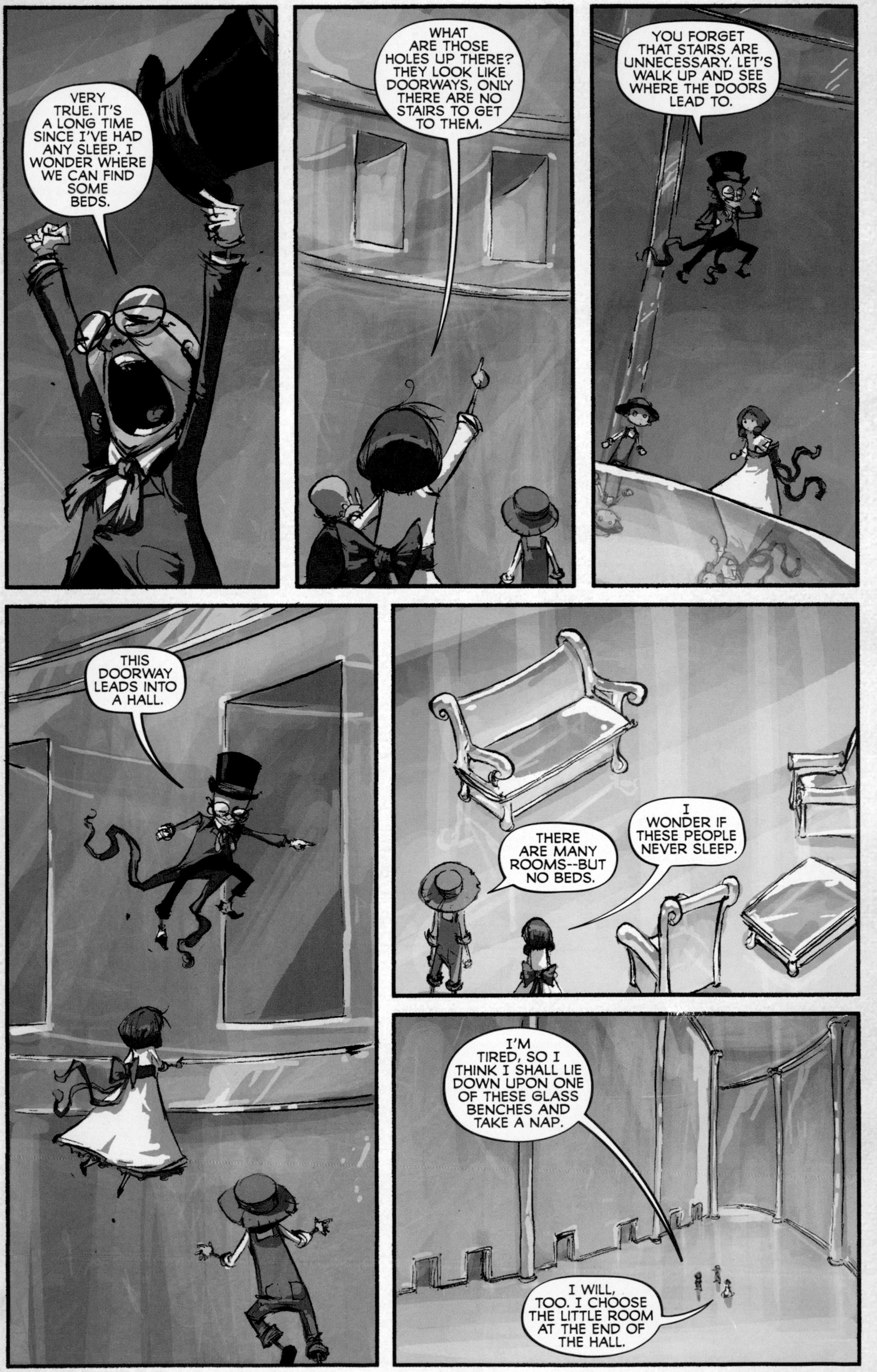
VERY TRUE. IT'S A LONG TIME SINCE I'VE HAD ANY SLEEP. I WONDER WHERE WE CAN FIND SOME BEDS.
WHAT ARE THOSE HOLES UP THERE? THEY LOOK LIKE DOORWAYS, ONLY THERE ARE NO STAIRS TO GET TO THEM.
YOU FORGET THAT STAIRS ARE UNNECESSARY. LET'S WALK UP AND SEE WHERE THE DOORS LEAD TO.
THIS DOORWAY LEADS INTO A HALL.
THERE ARE MANY ROOMS--BUT NO BEDS.
I WONDER IF THESE PEOPLE NEVER SLEEP.
I'M TIRED, SO I THINK I SHALL LIE DOWN UPON ONE OF THESE GLASS BENCHES AND TAKE A NAP.
I WILL, TOO. I CHOOSE THE LITTLE ROOM AT THE END OF THE HALL.

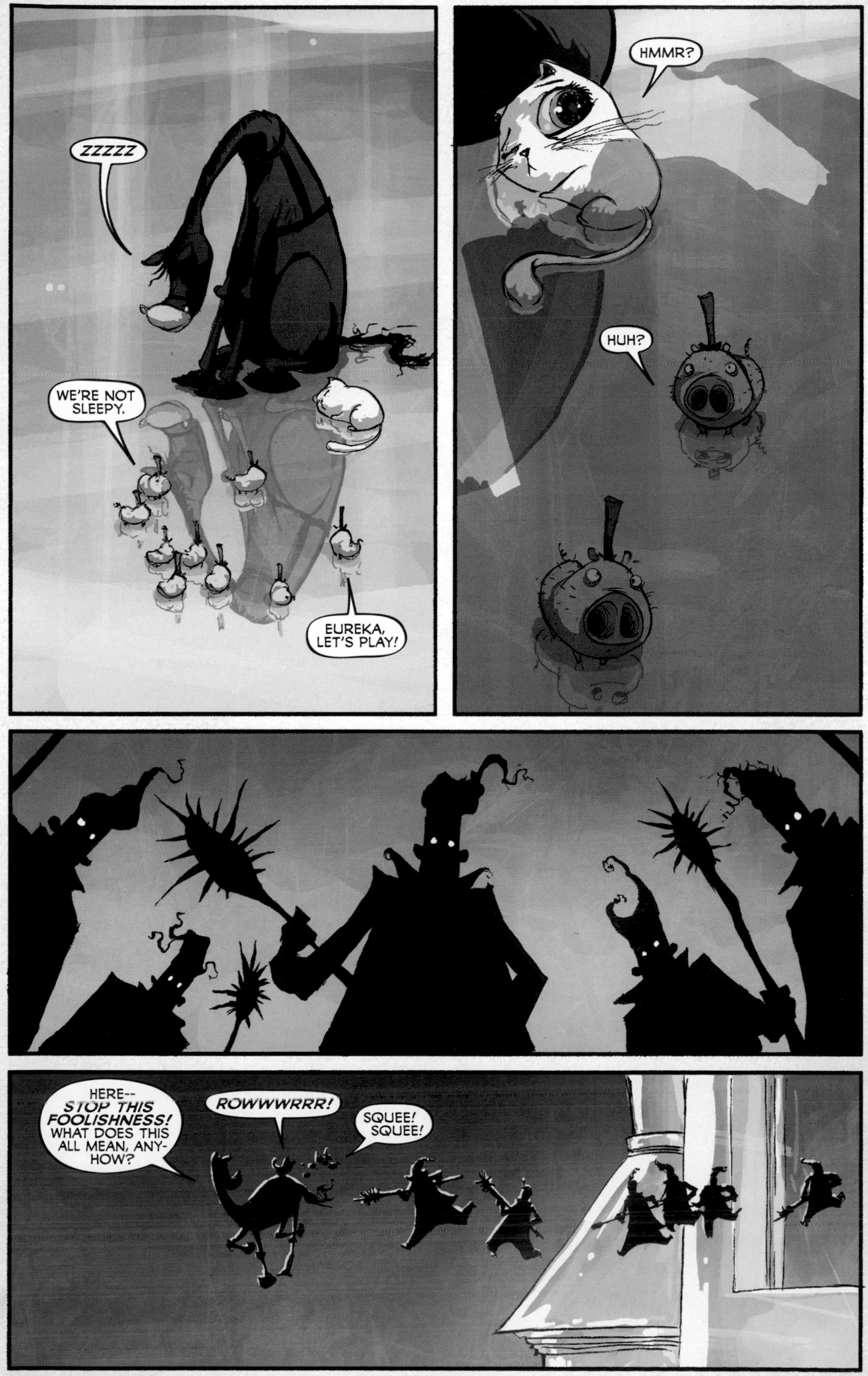
ZZZZZ
WE'RE NOT SLEEPY.
EUREKA, LET'S PLAY!
HMMR?
HUH?
HERE-- STOP THIS FOOLISHNESS! WHAT DOES THIS ALL MEAN, ANY-HOW?
ROWWWRRR!
SQUEE! SQUEE!

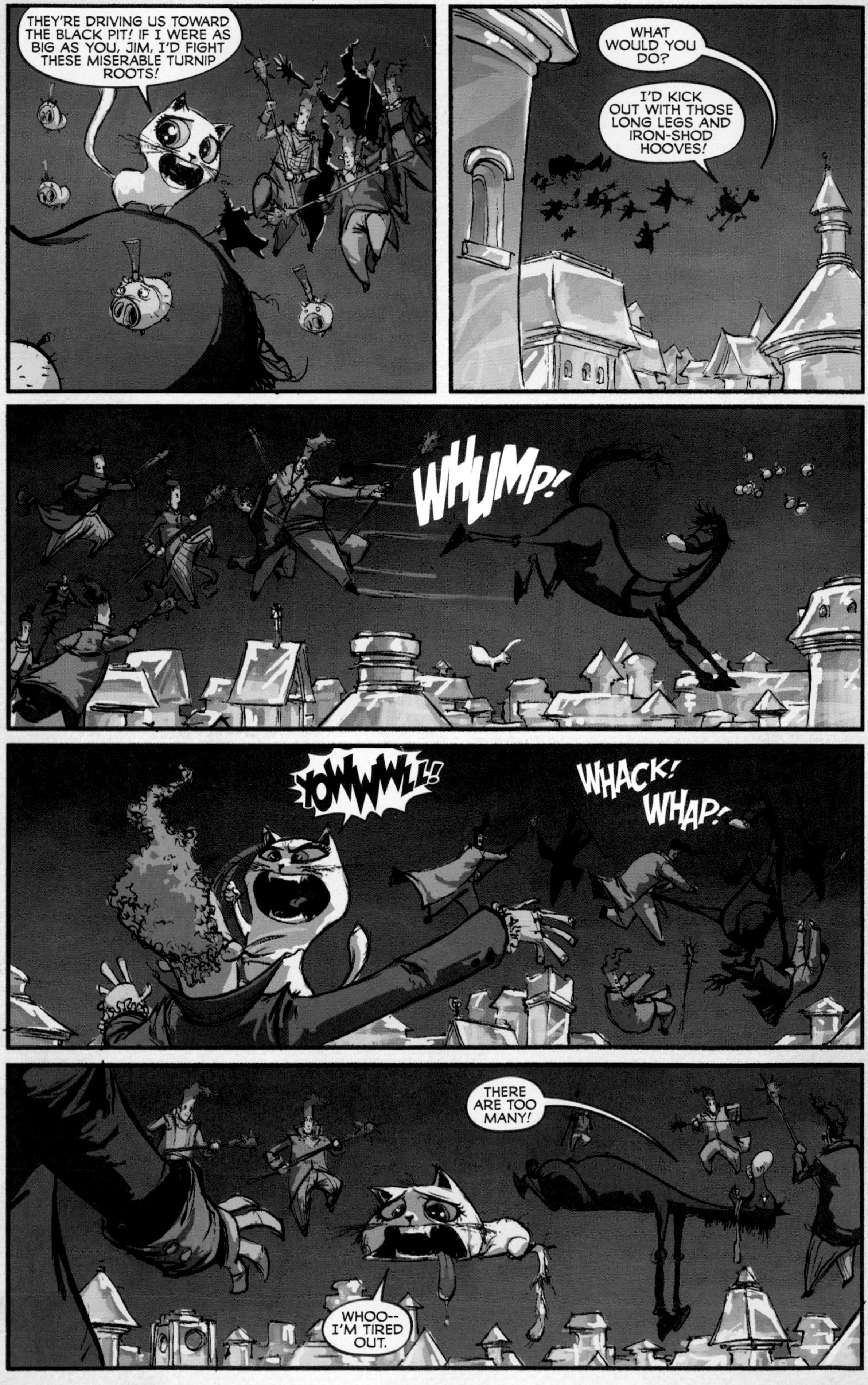
THEY'RE DRIVING US TOWARD THE BLACK PIT! IF I WERE AS BIG AS YOU, JIM, I'D FIGHT THESE MISERABLE TURNIP ROOTS!
WHAT WOULD YOU DO?
I'D KICK OUT WITH THOSE LONG LEGS AND IRON-SHOD HOOVES!
WHUMP!
YOWWWLL!
WHACK!
WHAP!
THERE ARE TOO MANY!
WHOO-- I'M TIRED OUT.

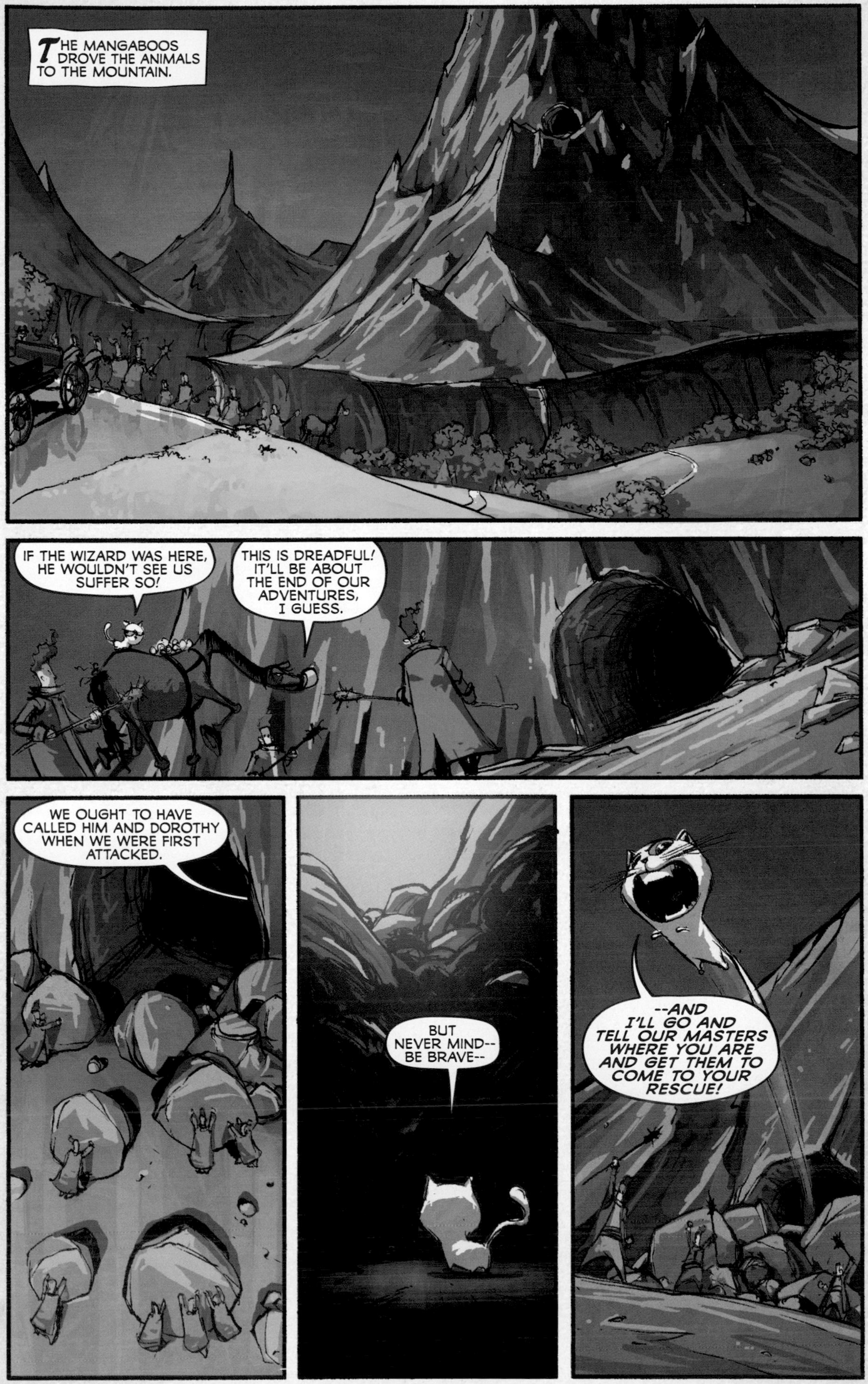
THE MANGABOOS DROVE THE ANIMALS TO THE MOUNTAIN.
IF THE WIZARD WAS HERE, HE WOULDN'T SEE US SUFFER SO!
THIS IS DREADFUL! IT'LL BE ABOUT THE END OF OUR ADVENTURES, I GUESS.
WE OUGHT TO HAVE CALLED HIM AND DOROTHY WHEN WE WERE FIRST ATTACKED.
BUT NEVER MIND-- BE BRAVE--
--AND I'LL GO AND TELL OUR MASTERS WHERE YOU ARE AND GET THEM TO COME TO YOUR RESCUE!

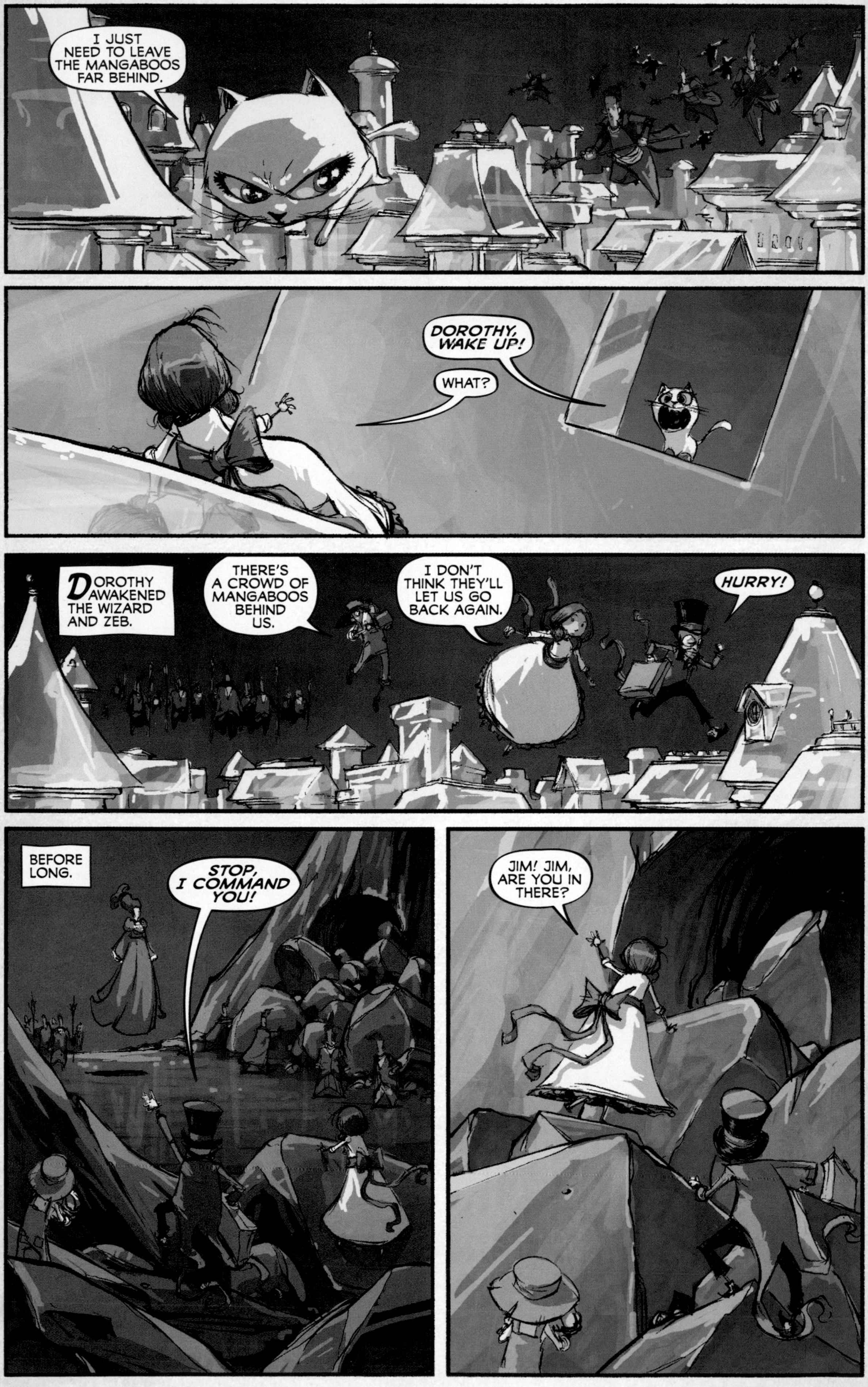

I JUST NEED TO LEAVE THE MANGABOOS FAR BEHIND.
DOROTHY, WAKE UP!
WHAT?
DOROTHY AWAKENED THE WIZARD AND ZEB.
THERE'S A CROWD OF MANGABOOS BEHIND US.
I DON'T THINK THEY'LL LET US GO BACK AGAIN.
HURRY!
BEFORE LONG.
STOP, I COMMAND YOU!
JIM! JIM, ARE YOU IN THERE?

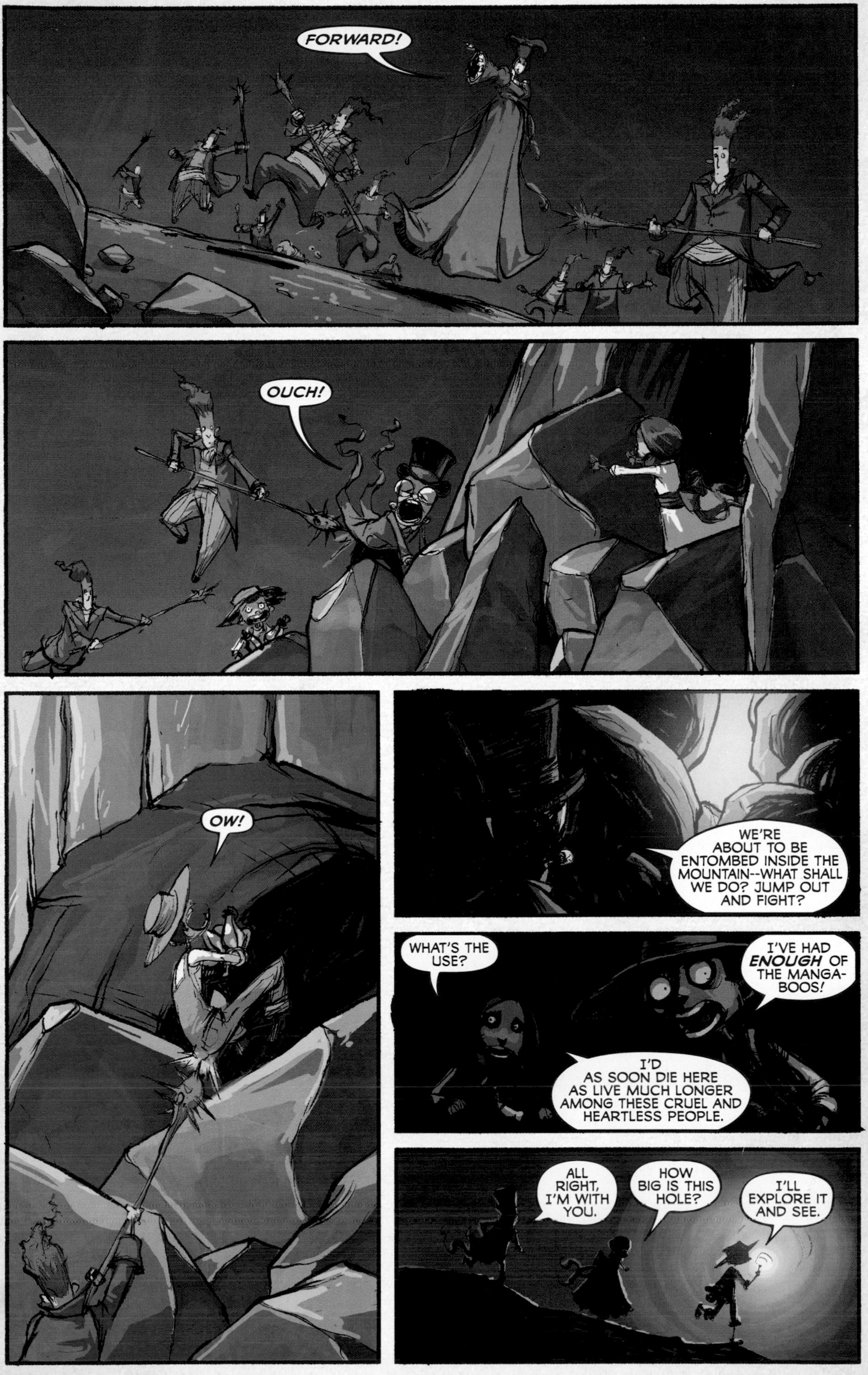
FORWARD!
OUCH!
OW!
WE'RE ABOUT TO BE ENTOMBED INSIDE THE MOUNTAIN--WHAT SHALL WE DO? JUMP OUT AND FIGHT?
WHAT'S THE USE?
I'VE HAD *ENOUGH* OF THE MANGA-BOOS!
I'D AS SOON DIE HERE AS LIVE MUCH LONGER AMONG THESE CRUEL AND HEARTLESS PEOPLE.
ALL RIGHT, I'M WITH YOU.
HOW BIG IS THIS HOLE?
I'LL EXPLORE IT AND SEE.

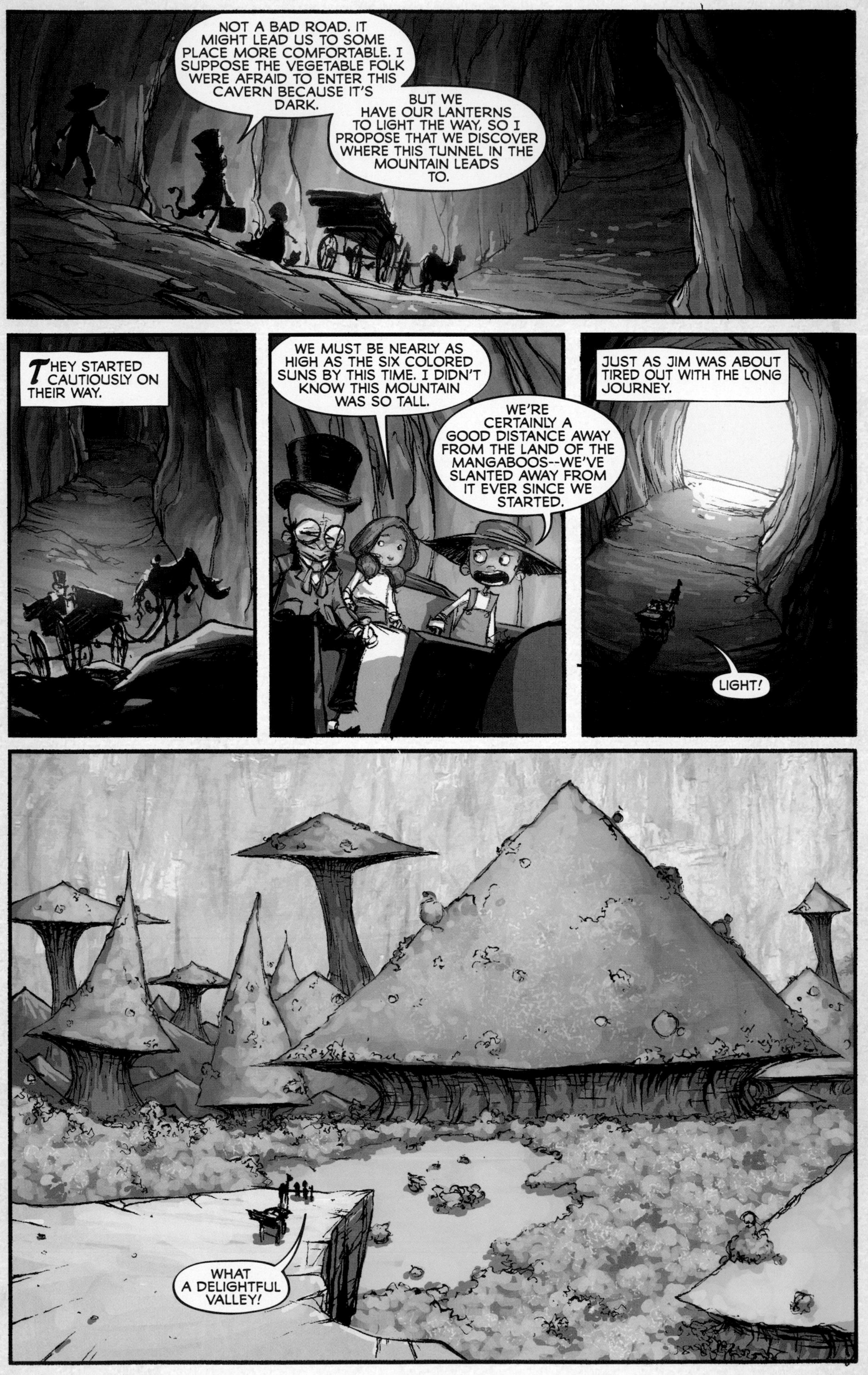
NOT A BAD ROAD. IT MIGHT LEAD US TO SOME PLACE MORE COMFORTABLE. I SUPPOSE THE VEGETABLE FOLK WERE AFRAID TO ENTER THIS CAVERN BECAUSE IT'S DARK.
BUT WE HAVE OUR LANTERNS TO LIGHT THE WAY, SO I PROPOSE THAT WE DISCOVER WHERE THIS TUNNEL IN THE MOUNTAIN LEADS TO.
THEY STARTED CAUTIOUSLY ON THEIR WAY.
WE MUST BE NEARLY AS HIGH AS THE SIX COLORED SUNS BY THIS TIME. I DIDN'T KNOW THIS MOUNTAIN WAS SO TALL.
WE'RE CERTAINLY A GOOD DISTANCE AWAY FROM THE LAND OF THE MANGABOOS--WE'VE SLANTED AWAY FROM IT EVER SINCE WE STARTED.
JUST AS JIM WAS ABOUT TIRED OUT WITH THE LONG JOURNEY.
LIGHT!
WHAT A DELIGHTFUL VALLEY!

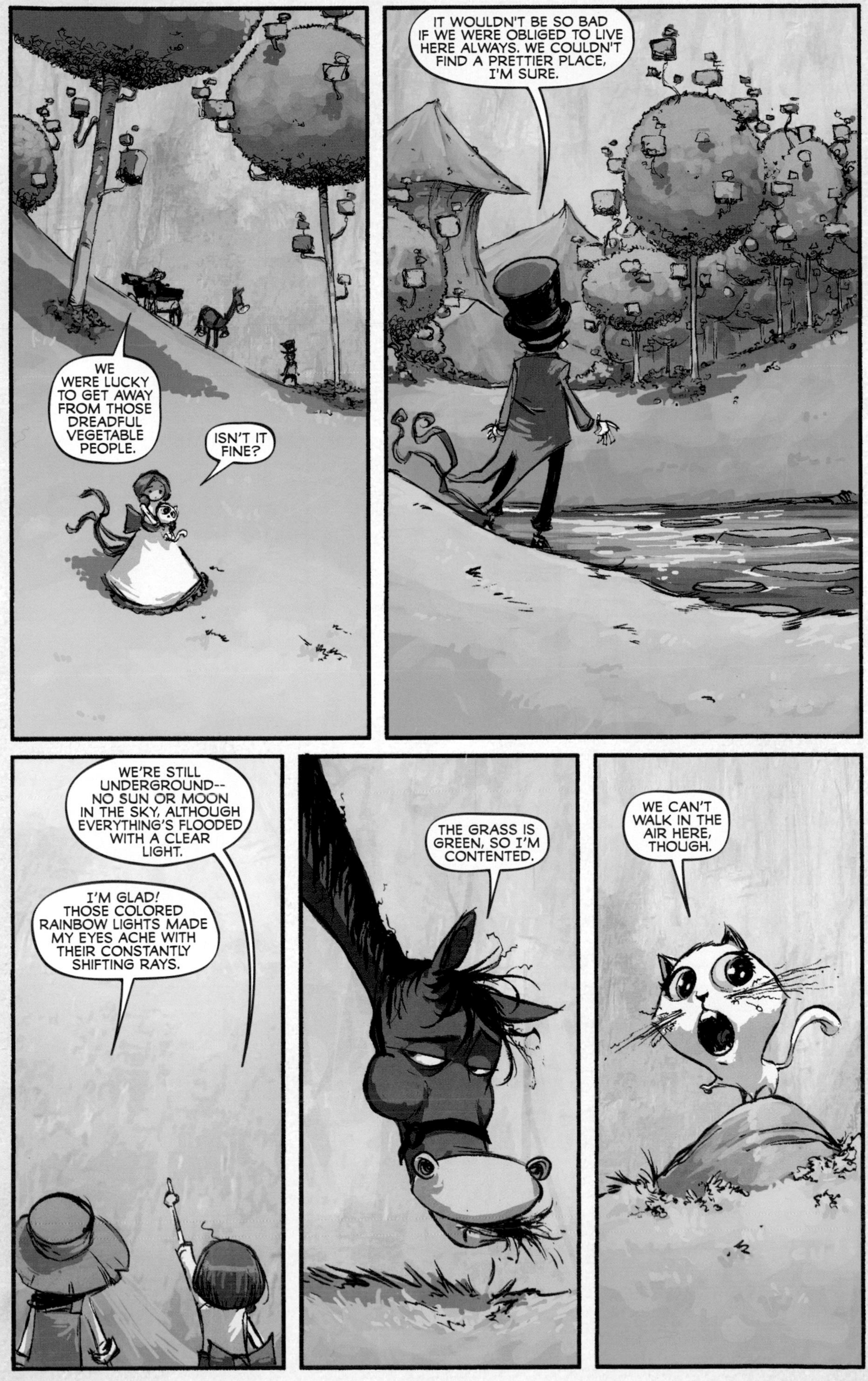
WE WERE LUCKY TO GET AWAY FROM THOSE DREADFUL VEGETABLE PEOPLE.
ISN'T IT FINE?
IT WOULDN'T BE SO BAD IF WE WERE OBLIGED TO LIVE HERE ALWAYS. WE COULDN'T FIND A PRETTIER PLACE, I'M SURE.
WE'RE STILL UNDERGROUND-- NO SUN OR MOON IN THE SKY, ALTHOUGH EVERYTHING'S FLOODED WITH A CLEAR LIGHT.
I'M GLAD! THOSE COLORED RAINBOW LIGHTS MADE MY EYES ACHE WITH THEIR CONSTANTLY SHIFTING RAYS.
THE GRASS IS GREEN, SO I'M CONTENTED.
WE CAN'T WALK IN THE AIR HERE, THOUGH.

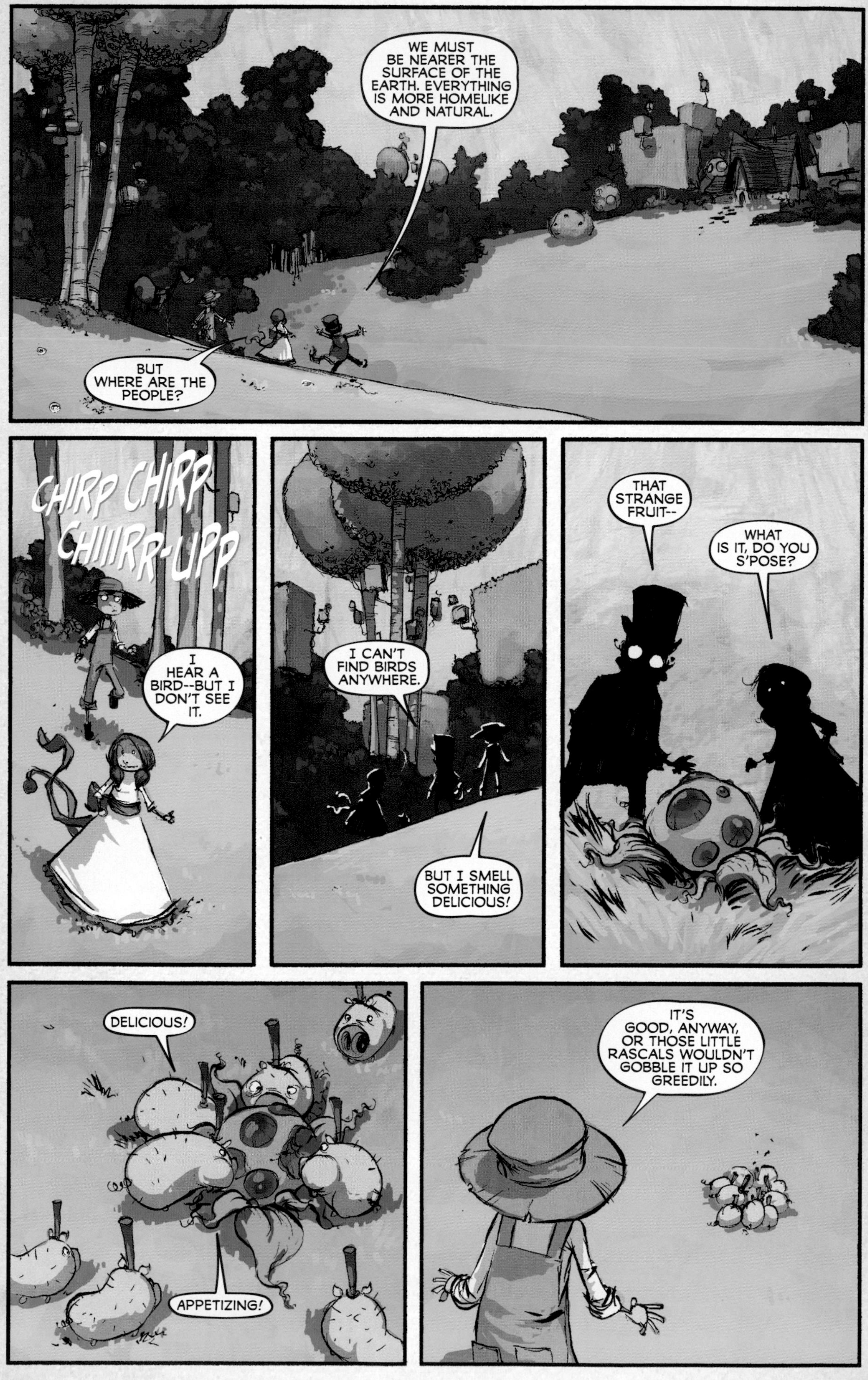
WE MUST BE NEARER THE SURFACE OF THE EARTH. EVERYTHING IS MORE HOMELIKE AND NATURAL.
BUT WHERE ARE THE PEOPLE?
CHIRP CHIRP
CHIIIRR-UPP
I HEAR A BIRD--BUT I DON'T SEE IT.
I CAN'T FIND BIRDS ANYWHERE.
BUT I SMELL SOMETHING DELICIOUS!
THAT STRANGE FRUIT--
WHAT IS IT, DO YOU S'POSE?
DELICIOUS!
APPETIZING!
IT'S GOOD, ANYWAY, OR THOSE LITTLE RASCALS WOULDN'T GOBBLE IT UP SO GREEDILY.

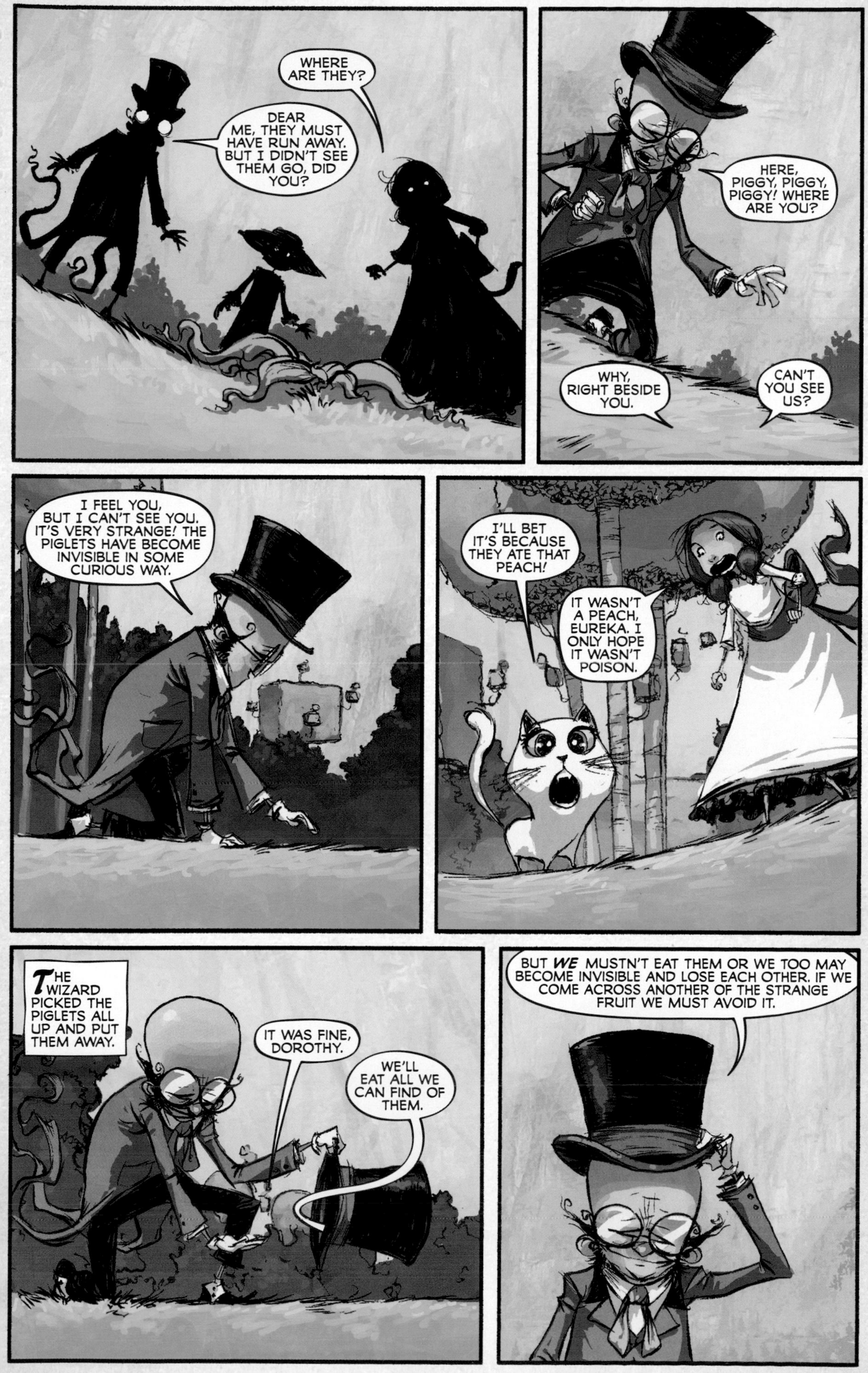
WHERE ARE THEY?
DEAR ME, THEY MUST HAVE RUN AWAY. BUT I DIDN'T SEE THEM GO, DID YOU?
HERE, PIGGY, PIGGY, PIGGY! WHERE ARE YOU?
WHY, RIGHT BESIDE YOU.
CAN'T YOU SEE US?
I FEEL YOU, BUT I CAN'T SEE YOU. IT'S VERY STRANGE! THE PIGLETS HAVE BECOME INVISIBLE IN SOME CURIOUS WAY.
I'LL BET IT'S BECAUSE THEY ATE THAT PEACH!
IT WASN'T A PEACH, EUREKA. I ONLY HOPE IT WASN'T POISON.
THE WIZARD PICKED THE PIGLETS ALL UP AND PUT THEM AWAY.
IT WAS FINE, DOROTHY.
WE'LL EAT ALL WE CAN FIND OF THEM.
BUT WE MUSTN'T EAT THEM OR WE TOO MAY BECOME INVISIBLE AND LOSE EACH OTHER. IF WE COME ACROSS ANOTHER OF THE STRANGE FRUIT WE MUST AVOID IT.

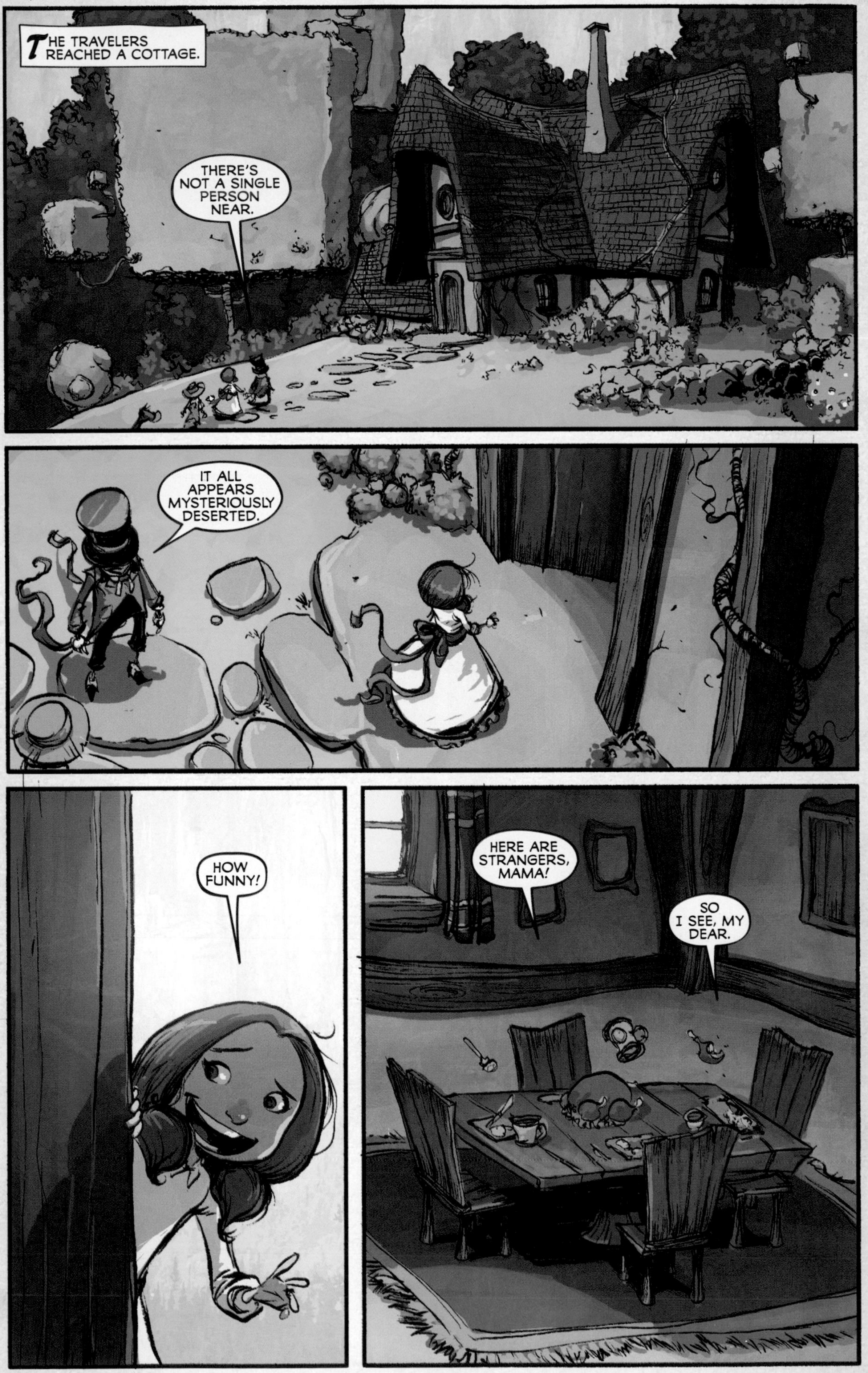
THE TRAVELERS REACHED A COTTAGE.
THERE'S NOT A SINGLE PERSON NEAR.
IT ALL APPEARS MYSTERIOUSLY DESERTED.
HOW FUNNY!
HERE ARE STRANGERS, MAMA!
SO I SEE, MY DEAR.

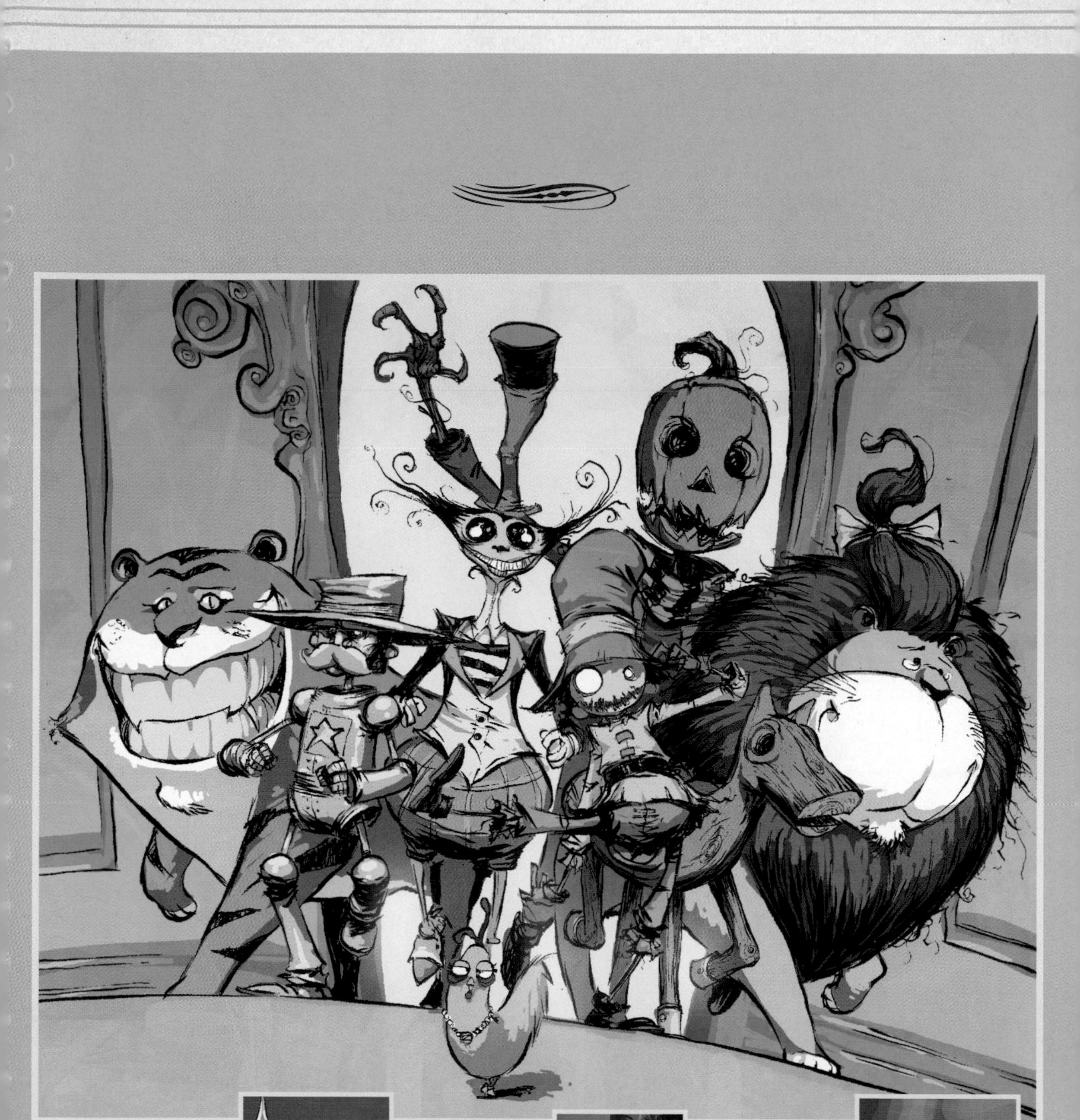
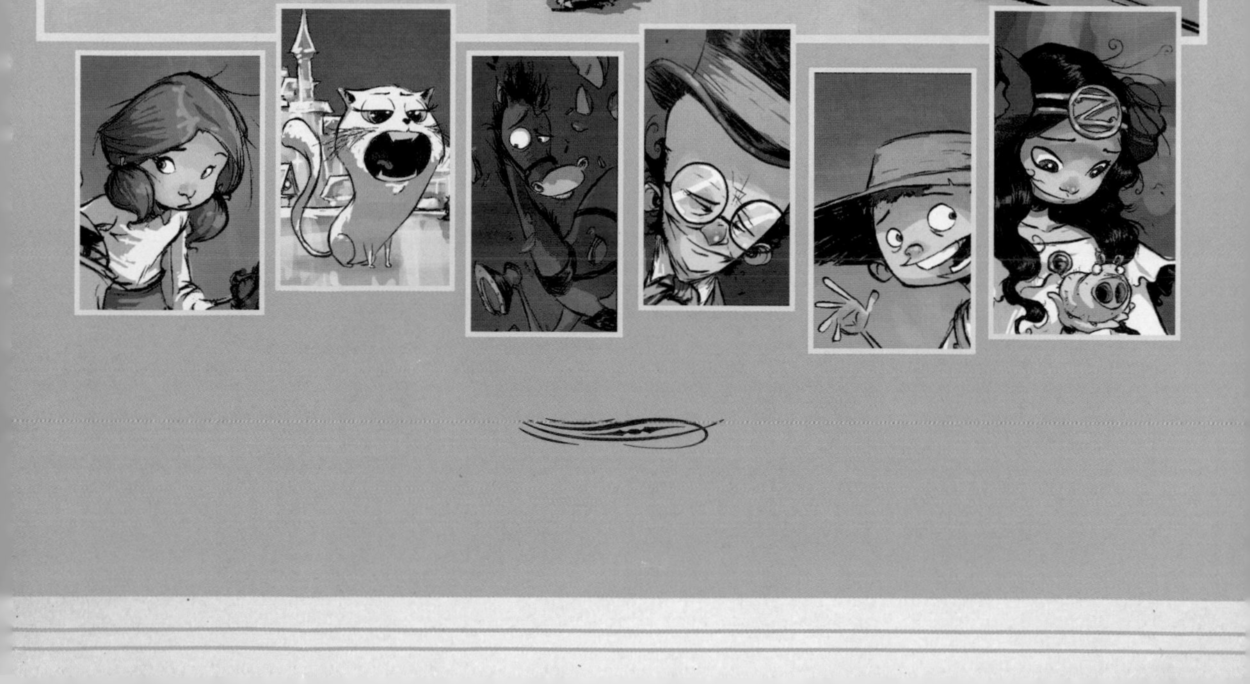

COLLECT THEM ALL!

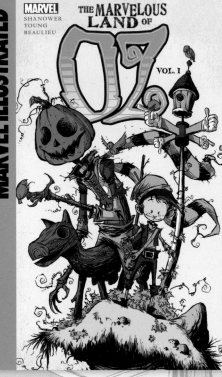

The Wonderful Wizard of Oz
Set of 8 books: 978-1-61479-225-3

The Marvelous Land of Oz
Set of 8 books: 978-1-61479-234-5

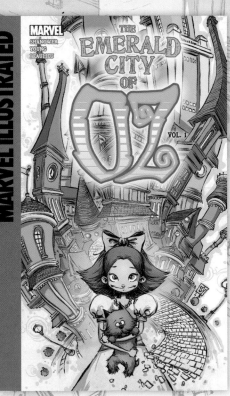

Dorothy and the Wizard in Oz
Set of 8 books: 978-1-61479-342-7

The Emerald City of Oz
Set of 5 books: 978-1-61479-351-9